Hades And Persephone

LIANA BROOKS

OTHER WORKS

ALL I WANT FOR CHRISTMAS

All I Want For Christmas Is A Reaper
All I Want For Christmas Is A Werewolf

FLEET OF MALIK

Bodies In Motion
Change of Momentum

HEROES AND VILLAINS

Even Villains Fall In Love
Even Villains Go To The Movies
Even Villains Have Interns
Even Villains Play The Hero (omnibus)
The Polar Terror

TIME AND SHADOWS

The Day Before
Convergence Point
Decoherence

SHORTER WORKS

Fey Lights
Prime Sensations
Darkness and Good

Find other works by the author at
www.lianabrooks.com

Hades And Persephone

INKLET #62

LIANA BROOKS

Inkprint
PRESS

www.inkprintpress.com

Print ISBN: 978-1-925825-64-0
eBook ISBN: 9798201314309

www.inkprintpress.com

National Library of Australia Cataloguing-in-Publication Data
Brooks, Liana 1982 –
Hades And Persephone
42 p.
ISBN: 978-1-925825-64-0
Inkprint Press, Canberra, Australia
1. Fiction—Fantasy—Romance 2. Fiction—Fairy Tales, Folk Tales, Legends & Mythology 3. Fiction—Short Stories

First Print Edition: July 2021
Cover photo © Cokacoka via Deposit Photos
Cover design © Inkprint Press
Interior art © Amy Laurens

HADES AND PERSEPHONE

THE CLOYING SMELL OF HOPE CLUNG TO the stone of the corridor like frost. Cloves and anise. Frankincense and *dathi*. They choked the air but could not cover the smell of death.

The Lord of the Dying moved over the stones in silence, magic warping the world so it was every place and no place at once.

People rushed by, fluttering blue robes dancing like frightened butterflies as they battled the inevitable. The plague held sway over the city. More dreadful than any war or famine was a disease fueled by magic. A disease only the high priestess could control.

It was she that Hades sought.

The other souls would find their way to the Underworld alone. But the priestess, soon to be his brother's bride, she would too soon pass from mortality into immortality and become a distant star out of his reach.

They had met long years ago when she was still a novice learning the litany of healing. A famine had crossed the continent and left the taste of ash in the air. The little healer had looked at him as she'd prayed over a small child and asked him to step away. She wanted the child to live.

He had taken an old soldier instead.

The child had lived to be a great scholar, beloved of the people.

The second time they met, war rode the land, making the rivers run with blood. The healer was older, blossoming into full womanhood, and this time she stood beside the bed of a tactician.

"Please, Lord of Death, leave him to defend the people. Let him save this city before he walks to your realm."

He had taken an old woman instead.

The third time they met as the king lay dying, his children squabbling over their inheritance. She was beautiful then, crowned by power and wisdom, filled with a god-touched soul that shone brighter than the sun. With a word she could raise the dead, bring spring and life, and conquer death. That time she had not asked him for a life, but for an hour of his time. Long enough for the king to declare an heir and bless his children.

He had listened.

So many times since then their paths had crossed. She the beautiful healer who brought light into darkness, and him the final silence of every dream. In those stolen moments and quiet hours they'd spoken of things only an immortal and a divinely blessed mortal could know. Of sunsets and magic. Of joy and hope. Of his brothers who ruled the mortal realm.

She was chosen. Beloved.

Worshipped. Fearful.

She did not love his brother. She did not wish to join the gods. She did not wish to leave her post. But the divine decree had gone out.

She had bargained for time.

The plague was the price.

He stopped at a door he knew was hers, the warmth of summer seeping through the wood even as cold carved the stone walls. "My lady?"

There was no reply.

Quietly, he unlatched the door and stepped into the room. Stepped fully into the mortal plane. For a moment becoming simply a man looking for the woman he loved.

She lay in the bed, dark hair sweat-soaked and sticking to her ashen face.

"My lady?"

Her eyes stared up unseeing. Her breathing was uneven.

Panic like he had never known swept across him. "My lady?" Hades fell to his knees beside her bed. The beautiful lady of flowers, the god-touched priestess of light was dying. He poured his magic across her, burning away every illness, bringing death to the plague that touched her.

Her pale lips twitched into a smile. "You cannot stop what I have done."

"You are dying?" It seemed unbelievable. "Tomorrow you will wed my—"

"I. Will. Not." Her teeth gleamed as her pain-filled smile turned victorious. "I will not be bought and sold. I will not take your brother's hand."

"What have you done?"

She turned and he could see the

pain stealing her strength. "A poison of man's making. Untouchable by your powers. Unknown to all but a few. And they are all dead except for me." Her words grew faint. "I am the last to know the cure. The last to die this way." Her hand struggled to reach for him. "Speak to me again. Tell me what you have seen."

He stood, angry and, for the first time in his immortal life, fearful. "I will not allow it. I will not allow you to crossover, to become a shade. Your name unspoken. Your memory burned away by the daylight."

"You cannot prevent it, my lord. I have done the unforgivable and denied the will of the great gods. They can have no power over me now." Her dark eyes filled with love. "For this moment alone, I am yours. Alone."

"If you are mine, then I have power over you." He could not lose her to the dark places. She'd become a wraith, a specter, a phantasm of memory and emotion. Never to laugh again, or speak to him, or plead for the souls of the dying.

He'd be alone without her. Bereft of her company. No one could ever replace her.

She turned. "I have enough power left for one last gift, my lord. What can I give the god of death?"

He took her hand. "Happiness?"

A delicate frown marred her beautiful face.

"Eternal happiness. Sunlight. Joy." The words choked him. This, he realized, was the sorrow mortals spoke of. The terror of losing someone they loved for the eternities. It was so much worse than he had ever dared imagine. "Stay with me. I love you."

Her smile was the light of a thousand dawns. "I would. My love, if there were a way, I would spend eternity with you. But my power is for healing, for sparing people, for helping them. I have no place in the lands of the dead. No way to walk in your realm except as one of your subjects. So many times you bowed to me, acquiesced to my every whim. It is time I bow before you."

"No."

Her eyes filled with pain.

"You will never bow before me. I would rather give up my immortality." His breath caught. He could. He could give her the crown of death. Make her Queen of the Dying.

Magic sparkled. "Do not. I will not let you leave me." The words were fueled by a power older than the gods. The power of a true priestess of creation.

He let his power slip, enfolding her, combining with her magic. Streams of light and darkness filled the air. Multi-colored sparks flew between them.

"I will never leave you, my love. My queen." He held out his hand.

She took it, the power filling her, the sparks lighting her from within. The mortal woman breathed in immortality and his queen stood. "Thank you."

Hades leaned forward, lips brushing hers. The warmth swept over him, changing him, bringing him the light and color that was not meant for death. Emotions filled him: joy, pride, cravings for her touch. Now he understood why men bargained with him at the sides of their wives. Now he knew why children wept. Why the wolves howled at the passing of their kin.

"There will be war," his queen whispered as she rested her head on his chest. "The gods will be angry."

"Gods may die in time, when they fall from favor, when the prayers go unsaid. But Death is eternal, born anew with every life. I am unending, and so, now, are you. Let the sun gods rage. You are something new. A goddess of second chances, forgiveness, rebirth, renewal, hope. It is to you that the forgotten will pray. The desperate and dying. Those seeking new lives and safety. Those damned by sorrow and depression. Those who need hope will come to you. Once I was the only one whom could give them rest, but now they have a Queen. A goddess. The fair Persephone, Queen of the Dead, goddess of light."

Her soft smile was his world.

"What is my queen's first desire?"

"First, I will save this city from the wrath of the gods so they will know in who they can trust. Then, my love, I will show you all the many things I have wished to do in those dark hours where we spoke but could not touch."

That smile would be his undoing, or his delight; he was eager to learn which.

Power flowed from her hand, sweeping across the city, bathing it in a golden light. The plague fell away. The trees bloomed. The grass sprung up new and fresh. The clouds rolled away, running from his queen.

She sighed happily. "It is enough. Now, my love," she took his hand, "show me your kingdom. Show me... everything."

THE MAKING OF
HADES AND PERSEPHONE

I always believed Persephone knew what she was doing when she ate that pomegranate.

The story of the woman who was called Kore (The Maiden) who ascended to the throne of the Underworld to become one of the most powerful forces of mythology has always fascinated me. I've written multiple variations. Sometimes Persephone is already a goddess, sometimes she is a mortal, sometimes she is something neither or both.

Whatever the case may be, here's to the Queen of Happily Ever After.

Read more by Liana Brooks!

FLEET OF MALIK: BODIES IN MOTION
CHAPTER ONE

THE PROBLEM WITH VACATIONS, Selena reflected as she adjusted her sweater outside Cargo Blue, was that reality was always waiting at the end. A quick search of the local security cameras found one that showed the peeling sunburn on her right shoulder blade.

Such was the curse of pale-skinned, ship-born Fleet personnel. Anytime she left the foggy belts covering the city of Tarrin, she barbecued like a shrimp, no matter how much sunscreen she applied. Otherwise, she'd flee even further from the Fleet Enclave and make her home on the equatorial beaches of the planet they were trapped on.

She panned the camera and checked her left shoulder. Black ink made a star-scape that disguised three silver scars as shooting stars. The painting covered her shoulder blade and part of her upper arm. As the artist had promised, the skin-paint had kept her from burning as much, though it still had the over-stretched feel of a burn. With a few adjustments, her uniform covered most of the temporary art; it would keep her from having to explain to her colleagues.

Her forearm warmed, a warning that someone was about to contact her through the tech implant tucked between her radius and ulna.

She hesitated too long and the call came through, a persistent ping against her skull as the phantom image of her best friend floated on the edge of her vision.

Selena turned off the visual receiver and answered. "Genevieve," she said with a smile as the image of her vivacious, red-headed friend appeared floating against the backdrop of landing gear that supported the grounded fleet.

A grounder would have thought she was talking to herself, but grounders wouldn't set foot near the neo-city-state of

Enclave. The rocky beach served as a city and tomb for the survivors of the last war.

"Selena!" Gen gushed. "Starcom to Selena. Where are you? I'm covering for now."

"Delayed, but almost there." Selena hoped Gen wouldn't hear the lie. She'd been standing in the shadows of the Enclave pub for nearly a quarter hour.

"The *Lorenza* could get here faster," Gen said, referencing a long-dead ship whose crew were found skeletonized at their stations. Gen blew hair off her face. "Stars above, you're an hour late. The whole fleet is flying faster than you."

Selena turned on her visual long enough to roll her eyes at her friend. "Ha, ha, funny. That joke needs to be forcibly retired." Sooner rather than later. The fleet couldn't fly without fuel, and the Malik system they were stranded in held precious few deposits of the orun crystals needed to power the ships.

"If you don't come," Gen said threateningly, "I will teleport to your apartment and drag you out in your pajamas."

"I'm not at home," Selena admitted. And she wouldn't have let her best friend come to her new house if she was.

Gen was smart enough to realize that the small palace Selena had bought in downtown Tarrin wasn't paid for by her official OIA salary. The paygrades for the Office of Imperial Affairs had last been updated when the Malik system was still in contact with the empire, making them 900 years out of date.

Technically, taking a second job wasn't treason, but there were enough people in the fleet who'd see it as a betrayal that keeping it secret felt right. Especially since Gen's captain was one who would scream the loudest.

Gen clapped. "Selena! Stop stalling yer engines and get in here. This isn't some Fleet Tribunal, just our friends. You, me, Carver. I left a message for Marshall. You know. People we like."

The light of understanding dawned. "Carver? This is so you can snuggle up to Perrin Carver without your parents watching?"

"Yes," Gen admitted, not looking the least bit contrite.

"You're only dragging me along so I can cover for you while you make out in a corner, aren't you?" She masked the relief with mock anger. At least Gen wasn't trying to set Selena up with one of her cousins. Or, ancestors forbid, Gen's handsy older brother.

Again.

Gen opened her eyes wide with an innocent smile. "Maybe."

"Gen!" Selena rolled her eyes. "Doesn't he have his own place?"

"Just the bachelor's dorm. The Carvers didn't have any ships except the shuttle his parents crashed in. Making out next door to Mom and Dad? No. And the BOQ? It's so tacky. You can hear everything through those walls."

Selena hid a smile. "I'll be there soon enough."

If Gen ever caught wind of how panicky the thought of a relationship made her, Gen would make it her life's goal to see Selena paired off. And there wasn't a man alive who she could imagine getting close to now.

Her implant helpfully pulled up an image of a tall, broad-shouldered, lean-muscled fighter with skin black as the night between stars and emerald-green eyes.

She pushed the memory away.

Lieutenant Commander Titan Sciarra was striking, intelligent, and had a body she'd cross battle lines for, but he was also out of reach. There was no point in chasing a man who wouldn't give her the time of day.

Another crew shuffled past her into the bar, black patches with silver fists on their shoulders.

It was getting harder to pretend she belonged in Enclave, with the fleet. Once upon a time, she'd known every crew's patch without thinking. She could name captains, their ships and their seconds by rote.

Now she would need to tap into the fleet's information nexus if she wanted to know who they were.

She stopped at the edge of the door to tug her lightest shields into place. A few minor adjustments would keep bugs away, keep beer off her clothes, and prevent anyone from hacking into her implant. They could still send messages, because disallowing that would have raised eyebrows. And they could still hit her. But she could always hit back.

Selena rolled her shoulders and strutted into Cargo Blue. It was a battle-field, but she was the last captain of the Caryll family, and she wasn't going down without a fight.

Whatever crew owned Cargo Blue probably hadn't had much of a decorating budget, but at least they'd stuck with a theme: oversized cargo boxes were piled up to make walls, seating, and tables. Olive-green safety webbing draped from the ceiling between blue lights. Fog used for fire drills on the ships pumped across the floor to hide the concrete beneath.

There was no bouncer at the door, but people were still hanging around the entrance.

As a rule, the fleet was cautious, and the young faces she saw belonged to fleet members who had never ventured outside their own crew more than a few times, even though the fleet had been grounded for nearly three years.

Tables to the left, bar ahead, dance floor to the right... and that meant the back half of the cargo hanger had been partitioned and karaoke would be in the back right corner. After a few minutes of weaving through the human crush, she found Gen, already sitting in Perrin Carver's lap and giggling.

"Selena!" Gen jumped up and hugged her. "I was beginning to worry!"

"How many people are in here?" Selena shouted over the music.

"Everyone under forty?" Gen laughed. With a small hand wave Gen put up a minor sound shield, muting the music. "People are going to stir crazy. Combine that with the anniversary—"

The anniversary.

Today.

The day the war had begun, the day the united fleet had died.

They'd been dying for four hundred years, well aware that the reserve of orun crystals was depleted and there was no way to move forward with the ships they had.

Old Captain Baular had seen the deposit of orun on the fifth planet as their saving grace. He'd get it even if it meant killing the grounders.

And, coward that he was, he'd ordered his grandson to lead the first attack instead of leading it himself.

That opening skirmish began and ended in the dark, with Titan Sciarra in the infirmary, and five Academy fighters mis-sing or damaged. But by lunch of the next day, every officer belonging to crews allied with the Baulars withdrew.

Seven months later, heated words turned to live rounds.

"Selena?" Gen asked quietly, placing a hand on her arm. "You didn't know the date, did you?"

"I was trying not to think about." If she had, she'd have cut her vacation to the islands early. Maybe even made her pilgrimage to the small cay where she'd ditched her stolen fighter after driving off the attack.

She rolled her shoulder, stretching the deep scars. "It snuck up on me."

"First round, we drink to the Lost Fleet, and all who've gone on to crew it. I'm buying," Gen said with a touch of forced joviality. "Carver's been making friends. Tell her, babe." She pushed Carver's shoulder.

Perrin Carver was tall, broad-shouldered man with shy, hazel eyes that hid a wicked sense of humor.

Selena's heart fluttered just a little at the memory of a time when she'd fancied herself in love with him. He'd been the ideal starsider: intelligent, good-looking, and charismatic. They'd been friends of a sort, but even that relationship had soured when she'd realized he'd been getting close to her so he could learn more about Genevieve Silar.

Carver nodded and held out his hand. "Hi, Selena. How are you?"

She tapped the back of his hand with hers, letting him test her shields. "Good. How's the Starguard?"

"Booming." The Starguard's commander smiled, white teeth flashing, but there was a tightness around his eyes. "Everyone hears about guardians being allowed outside the Enclave, or working with the Jhandarmi, and I'm drowning in recruiting requests. Captains of larger crews invite me to Captain's Mess so they can introduce me to their best and brightest. Half the time I can't tell if they want me to marry into the crew or take the fleetlings into the guard." His shield was still attached to hers, scanning her as he talked.

All he would get from her was polite interest. Her heartrate didn't spike or dip at the mention of the Jhandarmi. Her smile never flickered.

"Maybe you should lock down Gen," Selena said. "If you had a spouse, no one would try to get you to marry into the crew."

Carver and Gen shared a look, and Gen sent a ping of information that Selena's implant translated as an ongoing debate over crew name and a place to live.

Carver sent something similar; a picture of his bachelor's quarters and his one ship.

There was no room for them to marry and have a family.

"Enclave is a temporary solution," Selena said out loud. She'd lost the taste for communicating by implant years ago. "If we—"

A heavy hand wrapped around her waist as someone wearing too much cologne stepped far too close to her. "Hello, Selena."

Hollis Silar, one of Gen's many siblings, kissed her temple.

Simultaneously, Selena sighed, sent a shock through her shield to Hollis's hand, and elbowed him in the gut. "Hi, Hollis. I see you're still bathing in cologne rather than water."

He stepped away from her, an easy smile still in place.

It wasn't that Hollis was bad looking; plenty of women found him handsome.

It was that he was equally affectionate with every woman he saw and he couldn't keep a secret to save his life. Or anyone else's.

He'd chase anyone with a pretty smile and fell in and out of love a couple of times a day.

"Nice to see you too, Selena. Now, everyone, you're all going to look at me, smile, and laugh like I'm my normal, dashing self," he said, his smile never changing. "You haven't been paying attention, but I'm not a member of the Starguard for nothing. We're being watched. Now take your nice drinks from the waitress and keep your eyes on me."

Hollis nodded to the waitress and handed out four cups with bright purple liquid. "Bruised Stars all around. Guaranteed to make you giggle, or so the guy at the bar told me. Although he's a Seutaai, so take it with a shield in place." He handed Selena her drink with a smile, but immediately glanced over his shoulder.

"Big brother, who are we looking for?" Gen asked with a slow drawl. "Is it a friend who you might have forgotten to call back after a night out?"

Hollis shook his head. "No, I thought I saw some of the Lee crew. Make that, I'm certain of it."

Selena grimaced. "As long as Rowena isn't here."

"Did you call me?"

Startled, Selena looked up to the face of her least favorite woman: Rowena Lee.

"Hello," Selena said politely. "I see you're still alive. That's…"

Unfortunate.

She nodded and took a slug of her Bruised Star.

Rowena held up a tray of electric blue shots. "My crew thinks I can't out-drink anyone in this bar. I probably can't go toe-to-toe with alcoholics like the Silars here. But No-Shot Selena?" Rowena set the drinks on the table. "I can out-shoot you in the stars or on the ground."

Gen sucked in air between her teeth and sent Selena several urgent pings telling her to ignore the Lees.

Selena muted Gen. "I took plenty of shots in the war. As I recall, I disabled three of your big birds. *Bassi, Aryton, Theoano...* Bang, bang, bang." Selena mimed firing with her finger. "Three shots. Three silent ships."

"Not kills," Rowena said. "A whole war and you never blooded yourself."

That was it, the memory she didn't want to face; the time she'd almost taken Death's claim and risked killing someone outside of war.

"That's uncalled for," Hollis said, trying to step between them. "Selena, why don't we—"

Selena pushed Hollis aside and grabbed the first shot.

She tossed back the potent drink and shattered the glass on the table. "Go suck vacuum, Rowena. You're a pissant yeoman with no hope of command."

"I went to the Academy, same as you, Selena. I fought for the fleet." Rowena slammed a shot back. "You fought for the mud-lickers."

Selena took another shot as the first started to fuzz her judgement. "I prevented the Baulars from committing mass genocide and destroying the civilians along with the fleet."

Rowena took her second shot. A crowd was gathering and that seemed to feed her cruelty. "The Lees survived the war. We're still here. How many Caryll captains are there? Oh, right, one. Can you count that high, No-Shot? You have any idea how easy it would be for me to end you right now?"

Selena took the last two glasses and slammed them both back.

Gen pinged her, giving locations, counts, and identities of the Lee allies in the crowd.

Hollis stepped to her flank, ready to defend her.

She stood, anger burning through her veins. "Sure, your crew outnumbers mine. I guess on paper, it's not really a fair fight, is it, Rowena? But you were trained as a flight leader, and what do Carylls do? Hand-to-hand combat. Maybe I should thin your ranks, starting with one mouthy yeoman."

Keep reading! Head to:
www.inkprintpress.com/lianabrooks/
malik/bodies/

ABOUT THE AUTHOR

LIANA BROOKS lives a quiet, unassuming life somewhere in the Americas where she is absolutely *not* plotting to take over the world.

When she isn't being perfectly normal and average, Liana enjoys writing science fiction in every form, from sprawling space opera romances (the *Fleet of Malik* series) to the antics of a super-powered family (the *Heroes and Villains* series).

Liana also maintains a soft spot for paranormal romances. She writes the popular *All I Want For Christmas* novellas, including *All I Want For Christmas Is A Werewolf* and *All I Want For Christmas Is A Reaper*.

You can learn more about her and her books at www.LianaBrooks.com.

INKLETS

Collect them all! Released on the 1st and 15th of each month.

INKLET #055
Allure
AMY LAURENS

INKLET #056
The LIES We KNOW
LIANA BROOKS

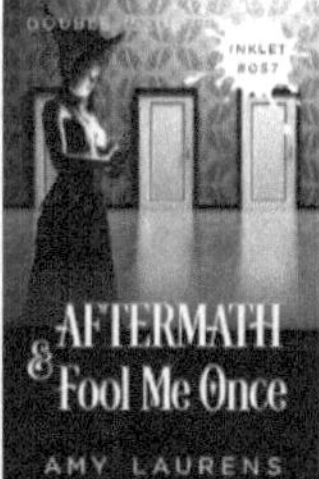
DOUBLE
INKLET #057
AFTERMATH & Fool Me Once
AMY LAURENS

INKLET #058
Purity
An Age Of Unicorns Story
AMY LAURENS

INKLET #059
Saved
AMY LAURENS

INKLET #060
A Kiss is the Secret
AMY LAURENS

INKLET #061
A Changing Tides Story
Fire Bright
AMY LAURENS

INKLET #062
Hades AND Persephone
LIANA BROOKS

INKLET #063
Just So Long As You're Happy
AMY LAURENS

INKLET #064
Theft Of A Lifetime
LIANA BROOKS

INKLET #065
Shoe
AMY LAURENS

INKLET #066
Published AUTHOR
LIANA BROOKS

DOUBLE ISSUE
INKLET #067
THE REMARKABLE INSIGHT OF JELLYBEANS & Understanding
AMY LAURENS

INKLET #068
Desperate Measures
AMY LAURENS

INKLET #069
Rock-a-bye
LIANA BROOKS

INKLET #070
the Other Carly
AMY LAURENS

INKLET #071
Bs By Bioluminescent Light
AMY LAURENS

INKLET #072
Even Villains Grant Wishes
A Heroes & Villains Story
LIANA BROOKS